Juliet Deacock was born in 1961 and brought up in London where she trained and worked as a nurse for many years before moving to Winchester, where she now lives with her family. She spent time in New Zealand which inspired her love of outdoor living and the countryside. She has recently left school nursing to pursue other interests. She enjoys cycling and many creative hobbies. This is her first published work.

Tatty Duck
A True Story

Juliet Deacock

AUSTIN MACAULEY PUBLISHERS™

LONDON ★ CAMBRIDGE ★ NEW YORK ★ SHARJAH

Copyright © Juliet Deacock (2019)

A CIP catalogue record for this title is available from the British Library.

ISBN 9781528976800 (Paperback)
ISBN 9781528976817 (Hardback)
ISBN 9781528976831 (ePub e-book)

www.austinmacauley.com

First Published (2019)
Austin Macauley Publishers Ltd
25 Canada Square
Canary Wharf
London
E14 5LQ

For Emily and Ollie.

Firstly many thanks to Shelley, Mike, Sam, Josh and Fergus for sharing their wonderful story. Also to my brilliant family, Simon, Emily and Ollie, for their support and encouragement and making me believe all this was possible.

HAMPSHIRE ENGLAND

In a special part of England, nestled in the Hampshire Downs
Winds the age—old Itchen River, where all of nature sounds.

The birds and ducks all calling, their song is 'oh so sweet'
The crystal waters sparkling, in the summer heat.

And this is where our story's set, starting one spring day
When mother Katie read the press and what it had to say:

"A little duckling needs a home," the local paper said,
"Abandoned by its mother. Will need to be hand–fed."

"It's really very tiny and just a few days old
If not looked after shortly, it will die out in the cold."

The Peck family lived in a cottage, a little way up stream
Katie, Mike and their three boys, excited and so keen.

They answered the advertisement, "We'll give it a home here."
Not once a second thought, a worry or a fear.

But Barny, their dear brown lab, would meet his new cute mate
How would that go, friend or foe? Let's hope it's love, not hate!

So baby duckling came to stay, was loved right from the start
Oh—so tiny and so dear, they hoped they'd never part.

This fluffy little duckling, now had three new brothers
It had a little bent—up beak quite different from the others.

But they found it was a poorly one, chesty and quite ill
They cuddled it and kept it warm, they didn't need a pill.

Soon the water and the food helped it get quite strong
'Hurray' it was much better, it chirped a little song!

On holiday they were due to go, but Sam would stay behind
So he became the special one as they were soon to find.

A boy or girl they did not know, the feathers would tell in time
Brown for girls and green for boys when they reach their prime.

It soon was known as Tatty Duck and this became its name
So much excitement for the Pecks and neighbours down the lane.

For a bed they used a cardboard box, a mop—head to it stuck
It felt all warm and cosy, just like a mother duck.

They put it by the oven to keep it warm and snug
And fed it little chick—crumbs, pecking from the kitchen rug.

A bucket in the garden was where Tatty learnt to swim
Waddling up a plank and then would suddenly jump in!

Now getting so much bigger, the hen—hut became its house
Into the cottage it would come squeaking like a mouse.

It would climb up onto Barny's back when lying on the floor
And help itself to their drinks, how they loved it more and more.

From bucket to the paddling pool and down to the river they'd go
Tatty and all the family, with Barny still in tow.

The paddling pool still so much fun, in circles it would swim
Hilarious and total joy when all the boys got in!

When Tatty got its grown—up feathers, 'twas time to learn to fly
Being a pilot, Mike declared, "I will give it a try."

He ran around the garden flapping arms up in the air
So funny did he look, all Tatty did was sit and stare!

With all the feathers grown now, clearly a girl was she
Such a special and unusual one as other ducks would see.

Eventually the day arrived, when to the river she'd fly
And there to stay all on her own, as many days went by.

One cold day Sam walked the dog, wrapped up in coat and scarf
On seeing Sam she followed him home – oh how it made them laugh!

Sometimes she'd pop back to the house and make her presence known
But happily she's settled now, the river's her new home.

Not seen for many weeks, the neighbours all so sad
Mike saw a pretty lady duck with the bent—up beak she'd had.

Surrounded by her feathered friends, so grown—up she'd now become
Swimming happily down the river, she was having so much fun!

Her funny little bent–up beak didn't bother her at all
In fact she was quite proud of it, she'd stand up straight and tall.

Whilst Mike was sad he had to smile, she'd brought them many joys
To know they'd raised a healthy one, just like their big strong boys.

So Tatty we hope you'll find a mate and our job will soon be through
And maybe have your own baby ducks to love like we love YOU!!!

The adventures of Tatty Duck will continue in
Tatty Duck Grown Up.